# CHRISTMAS WITH MOTHER GOOSE

The Playmore/Waldman Bug Logo® is a registered trademark of Playmore Inc., Publishers and Waldman Publishing Corp., New York, New York

Published by Playmore Inc., Publishers and Waldman Publishing Corp., New York, New York

Copyright © MM Playmore Inc., Publishers and Waldman Publishing Corp., New York, New York

Printed in Canada

"Hi, Elves! I have a letter for Santa Claus."

**Children from many countries write letters to Santa . . .**

"It's an invitation to a Christmas party
in Mother Goose Land."

"That sounds like fun!" says Elf Bedkin.

"Good day, Mother Goose!"

"Hello! I'm Little Jack Horner, and I'm eating my Christmas pie."

Jack Sprat and his wife are eating . . . as usual!

"Polly, put the kettle on, and we'll all have tea."

"After tea, we'll give out the gifts."

The Cat and the Fiddle get a new tape recorder . . .

. . . and the Cow that jumped over the moon gets an astronaut suit.

**There's an insect-proof tent for Little Miss Muffet.**

Simple Simon is happy with a pie of his very own.

Mary and her Little Lamb are thrilled with friendship lockets.

Humpty Dumpty loves his new safety net.

Mittens with ribbons are for the Three Little Kittens.

And here's a new see-saw for Margery Daw.

What a great gift for Rock-a-Bye-Baby — a parachute!

Baa-Baa Black Sheep loves his new cart
for carrying his wool.

Here's a perfect gift for Jack and Jill — crash helmets!

This is just what Little Bo-Peep needs —
a puppy to help her watch her sheep.

Little Boy Blue thanks Elf Bedkin for his new horn.

Peter Pumpkin-Eater and his wife love their new television set.

The Old Woman Who Lives in a Shoe . . .

. . . gets a wagon full of toys and food for all her children.

**Elf Bedkin brings the Crooked Man a crooked present.**

Old Mother Hubbard now has a cupboard full of goodies.

"Before we leave, I have one last gift — a special one."

"It's for Mother Goose, and it's a . . .

. . . very beautiful book of Mother Goose stories.''

Merry Christmas to all, and to all a good night!

SR-SR/G426-10/I3799/32